The Curse of Adolf Hitler's Pocket Watch

The Curse of Adolf Hitler's Pocket Watch

Peter J. Moore

Peter Moore Publications

Peter Moore Publications
Calle D'ibi No. 14, El Campello,
Alicante 03560, Spain

First edition published by
Peter Moore Publications
Copyright (c) 2011 Peter J. Moore

First edition 2011

ISBN: 978-0-9569098-4-8

Printed and bound in Great Britain by
Lightning Source UK Ltd,
Chapter House, Pitfield, Kiln Farm,
Milton Keynes MK11 3LW

About the author

Peter J. Moore was born in 1939, just three months prior to the outbreak of the Second World War. He grew up in the East End of London with the sounds of sirens and bombs. His first school and home was demolished with the constant bombings before he was evacuated, so it is natural that he has taken an interest in all aspects of the conflict and those directly involved.

As a keen independent traveller and yachtsman he has written several magazine articles for motorhome, camping and yachting magazines. He has published one non-fiction book *Moore's Way* (Trafford Publishing, 2008) to which a sequel is in preparation. This is his first novel.

Peter lives on the Costa Blanca in Spain.

Contents

Acknowledgements

I would like to say thank you to Sandra Clegg, my partner, for her dedicated assistance and support in completing this book, and to my son Robert and his wife Alison for proofreading the manuscript and their encouragement.

Prologue

London, 1984

ETECTIVE SERGEANT Dickie Davis had just started eating a not-too-edible ham and tomato sandwich when the call came though: a serious incident in a pawnbrokers in Cable Street in the East End.

Accompanied by WPC Jill Fallgate, he drove to the crime scene as quickly as the pre-rush-hour traffic permitted, complaining throughout the journey about his lunch and London cabbies who resolutely ignored the police siren and refused to get out of his way.

Old Manny Rosenberg had run the shop for many years. He was well respected by the poorer residents in the area who saw him as the man who would take virtually anything in exchange for cash, giving them the opportunity to raise money when funds were low and get their items returned when they had spare cash. They would often repeat the cycle of exchange time and time again, and Manny only charge a small fee.

As the police car stopped outside the shop, the first thought that entered Davis's mind was that the crime scene was completely ruined by the number of people crammed inside. Behind the counter's grill bars an elderly woman was huddled, sobbing uncontrollably and being consoled by a younger woman.

A bare 40 watt light bulb swung slowly above the body of an elderly man sitting in a chair. Both wrists and ankles had been bound to the arms and legs of the chair.

He had been badly beaten. Both eyes were black and swollen. His nose had been broken and blood streaked down his face; there were also cigarette burns on his body. He had been severely tortured before his throat had been slit and his clothes were covered in blood.

In the rear of the shop a stocky young man in his twenties, whom Davis ascertained was Manny's son Alan, was searching through cabinets very quickly and without much care, frantically trying to establish why his father had been so brutally murdered, leaving his sister Sonya to comfort his hysterical mother, Rose.

Until now, Alan had been unable to find any reason for it. The cabinets that contained many items of value – including gold rings and brooches of silver and gold with precious stones – remained untouched. The safe had not been opened and the only items the villains seemed interested in were the pledge tickets, which were scattered all over the floor – and, as if to underline this, the pledge book was missing. In it were recorded the date, item pledged, name and address of client: and the amount paid for the pledge.

'*Why on earth would anyone want a pledge book so much that they would torture and murder for it?*' Davis murmured to himself as he left the pawn shop, having briefly interrogated the grieving family and leaving them in Jill's capable hands as he drove back to the police station.

He had enquiries to make, some thinking to do – and a sandwich to finish.

1   The Promise

PADDY O'BYRNE was feeling rather pleased with himself after pulling off a great win on the gee gees. It gave him the opportunity to return to Ireland for his daughter's wedding in Glenamaddy, a village just east of the border of County Galway.

After informing the neighbours of his departure and expected return date he locked up his council flat in east London and made his way to Euston Station to catch the boat train for Ireland.

It was overcast and starting to rain when he arrived in Glenamaddy – and much cooler than London for September – but Paddy wasn't in the slightest bit bothered: he was far too excited about meeting up with the family and his son Jamie, who had an important job with the Hilton Hotel Group.

All the family were so delighted that he had been able to make the crossing for his daughter's wedding and gave Paddy a warm welcome, as there had been times when the family thought he would not make it because of his health. He had been to the doctor recently with his heart, which had always been a problem and was made worse by his drinking and smoking. The doctor had warned him to stop, but Paddy ignored the advice. There was also the question of his finances, which seemed to be controlled by his visits to the bookmakers.

If the bookies were kind and friendly, everyone would know, but if they were being unfriendly, as Paddy would put it, he would keep a low profile. He sat now with a drink in one hand and the inevitable cigarette in the other, while he watched his children. Jamie and his sister Kathleen were as different in appearance as chalk and cheese. Where she was a diminutive five foot green-eyed redhead – he was six foot four in his socks, clean-shaven but with a mop of dark curly hair that any girl would die for. His twinkling blue eyes masked a keen intellect and a sharp brain.

* * *

Kathleen's wedding to Brendan was a great success. The festivities continued for three days, by which time Paddy had been taken ill after over-indulging in booze, cigarettes and cigars.

Jamie had enjoyed the wedding enormously but was now very worried by his father's condition. When he looked at his father in the small bedroom of Kathleen and Brendan's tiny cottage he just knew that Da would not survive until the doctor's arrival – it would take the doctor more than four hours to get here.

Paddy was well aware of this: his mind had always been that much fitter than his body. He was not afraid of dying as he had faced death on many occasions. His wife had died ten years ago and most of his friends had now passed on. He explained all this to Jamie, adding, as he became weaker and his voice softened, that he had nothing of value to leave to the family.

Instead he had a request to make. He wanted Jamie make a solemn deathbed promise.

'Jamie, lad, I need you to swear to me that you'll keep my agreement with Manny Rosenburg.'

Jamie bent closer to his father to hear his whispered words. 'Tell me, Da. What about Manny?'

Paddy took a firm hold of his son's hand and looked into his eyes. 'You must fulfil the promise I made to him, whatever happens.'

'I promise. If it is possible, then I'll do it for you.'

Paddy eased back on his pillows and sighed. 'Well, my boy, this is what happened.

'Many years ago I came by an old pocket watch. It was made of solid gold, which I thought would be of value to somebody. As time passed I learned that the watch was of no value – nobody wanted it, in fact it was hated by most people who looked at it. Some people even spat at it. So as no one wished to buy it, it seemed completely worthless.

'Until, that was, one day when my funds had reached rock bottom and the bookies were being unkind. In desperation I took the watch to Manny on the slim chance that he might accept it as a pledge – which he did for almost anything.

'When Manny saw the watch his hands started to tremble and his eyes grew large behind his wire-rimmed glasses. He dropped the watch onto his desktop, raised both his hands above his head and muttered something in Yiddish.

'"Why have you brought this thing to me?" he asked.

'"For a pledge of course and no other reason. What will you offer for a loan?" I replied.

'"If I did not know you as well as I do I would throw you out my shop. Bringing this thing to me, of all people!" he shouted.

'I did not want to upset the old fella so I just asked for the watch back, saying I was sorry.

'"No one likes the damned thing," I said, "but I cannot understand you not wanting to accept it as a pledge."

'"No one likes it, you say?" Manny retorted. "Well, there are people who would like it and pay a lot of money for it but they must never have it. Not even over my dead body," he added, wringing his hands together.

'"Who are they?" I asked with curiosity.

'"You ask a Jew, that! Never you mind," he replied. "I will accept this as a pledge on one condition: that you make a solemn promise to me that you will never sell or pledge this watch to anyone but me – or if I am dead, to another Jew."

'"How much is the pledge?" I asked.

'He made a very generous offer for something I felt was worthless, so I agreed to the old man's demand. Years have passed since I made that promise to Manny, and the watch has been passed between us time and time again. He was always as good as his word, even up to a few weeks ago when I pledged the watch again to Manny for the stake on the gee gees, which gave me the very best win I have ever had. I rushed to Manny's shop to redeem the watch because I knew he really didn't like it and paid him more than he asked for the pledge.'

'Why on earth did he want you to sell the watch to him if he hated it so much?' asked Jamie.

'When I asked the same question, he told me, "That's between me and my maker." I just think that he didn't want anyone else to have it, even though he did not really want it himself. That is my solemn pledge and promise to him, and I cannot rest unless I am sure it will be fulfilled. So I am asking you, Jamie my son, to promise your poor old Dadai that you will do this last thing for me. Promise me now, on my deathbed.'

'I promise, Da, but where is the watch?'

'It's in the inside pocket of my jacket, hanging over there on the bedroom door.'

Jamie crossed the room and took the small red leather case from his father's jacket. Turning, he saw Paddy lying in the bed, his eyes closed as if he were peacefully asleep. He had slipped into death with his son's promise in his ears and a lightness in his heart.

Jamie knelt at the bedside. 'Rest easy, Da. I will take care of everything.'

* * *

This was the first time Jamie had experienced the death of anyone close to him. He was working abroad when his mother passed away and, as a young boy growing up, he had always been closer to his father. So this final moment with his father, knowing that he would never be able to speak with him again, came as a great shock, although Paddy had not been in the best of health for several years. But as all the family's thoughts, at this time, were with Kathleen's marriage, and the happiness of the young couple, Jamie waited for the newly weds to leave for their honeymoon before breaking the news of his father's death.

When the doctor arrived he informed the undertaker and arrangements for the funeral were completed. Jamie now had some time to be alone and reflect on the past relationship he had with his father.

He went into the lobby and pulled on an old pair of wellies; then, donning a large trench coat, he stepped out into the overcast day.

As Jamie wandered through the familiar countryside, he found himself retracing the steps he had taken on many occasions with his father as a child, leading to the raised bogs of Lough Lurgeen and Glenamaddy Turlough. His father knew these bogs very well, and the safe routes to cross them, and had passed this knowledge on to Jamie, warning him of the dangers of getting a pathway wrong and stepping into a sinking bog, never to be seen again, as many had done in the past.

Some bogs had been drained, or nature had changed their structure, to reveal their victims, who were often well preserved. Many stories were told: there was the couple found in a car that had left the road and disappeared into a bog; or the couple who had been found with hands and feet tied, presumably deposited in the bog as a punishment for a crime they had committed.

Although Paddy warned Jamie about the bogs, and the safe routes to use, he had also pointed out their beauty —their rich plant life, flora and fauna, and the wide variety of migrating birds that inhabited the area.

Jamie was surprised at how easily he remembered the safe routes his father had pointed out to him long ago. He now felt calm and ready to cope with the funeral which was due to take place at St Patrick's Church, where the family had always been buried, in a reserved plot of land After the service he would preside at the wake organised for his father at Kelly's shebeen.

* * *

After the funeral Jamie returned to London and decided to visit his father's council flat before going home to his mews house in Chelsea. He intended to settle Paddy's affairs as soon as possible – and his most important task now was to pass the watch over to Manny, just as he had promised his Da.

On arriving at the council flat he was greeted by the next-door neighbour, who offered her condolences after hearing of his father's sad passing. She also informed him that she had entered his father's flat to check that everything was satisfactory for his father's return, only to find that it had been burgled. Nothing seemed to be missing and it was a mystery how the criminals had got in because there was no evidence of a forced entry. The police informed her that they had recorded it as yet another statistic.

The lady thought it must have been 'druggies'. 'They get in and pinch anything for a fix.' She was about to leave but turned her head and added, 'This is the third piece of bad luck I have heard this week – what with your Dad, dying, his house wrecked and poor old Manny Rosenberg murdered ... whatever is London coming to? It must be all these foreigners.'

Jamie was then appalled to discover that the flat had been totally ransacked: every drawer and cupboard had been emptied onto the floor, the bed had been turned upside down; and the place was a complete mess.

Yet as he looked around he realised that nothing seemed to be missing – not even his dad's TV or video machine, prime objects for druggies, he thought.

It took Jamie around two hours to restore the flat to normal and make himself a cup of tea. Then he sat contemplating how he was going to clear the flat. The local council, had a list of potential tenants for these flats. He would also need to notify the local services of his father's death. The neighbours promised to remove most of the furniture for him but the clothes and knickknacks could go to the Church.

His thoughts now turned to the promise he had made to his father. Manny was dead so he could not pass the watch on to him, but as his father said, if this was the case, the watch must be passed on to or sold only to another Jew who would accept it.

Until now, too much had been happening for Jamie to consider opening the case which contained the offending watch. So he took the small red leather case from his pocket and pressed the spring catch button, allowing the top to fly open.

Adolf Hitler's face, engraved on the front of the watch above a small swastika, stared up at him, with the date 20.04.1940 underneath.

Jamie was shocked. He quickly turned over the heavy, solid gold Hunter pocket watch. He opened the front and found a white face with gold hands and numbers, together with the gold motif of Breitling watches with the sign of the swastika underneath.

Inside the back cover was engraved a German inscription:

Glüchlich Fünfzigsten Gerburtstag
Adolf Hitler
Mein Fuhrer
von
Martin Bormann
20.04.1940

Jamie's job required him to speak four languages fluently. Translated into English, the inscription read: '*Happy 50th Birthday, Adolf Hitler, My Leader, from Martin Bormann, 20.04.1940*'.

The watch was supported with a heavy gold chain and a fob shaped like an eagle clutching a swastika in a ring, similar to the one on top of the Brandenburg Gate in Berlin during the war. On the back was an engraving of the Eagle's Nest Fortress.

Jamie was truly horrified at what he was holding in his hands. It was understandable that no one wanted anything to do with it and that Manny Rosenberg wanted to make sure it didn't get into the hands either of neo-Nazis or anyone who could make money out of it. How was he going to fulfil his promise to his father now that old Manny had been murdered?

He would have to find a Jew who would accept the watch from him – but who and where? Perhaps his girlfriend Rachel might have some ideas. She was half-Jewish and maybe she would be able to offer some advice on how best he could dispose of the watch and keep his deathbed promise.

2   The Quest

ACHEL LIVED in a house in Stanmore and Jamie had a luxury mews house in Chelsea. It was their mutual professions that brought them together and yet kept them apart. Rachel was the marketing director of a frozen food company and as they both needed to travel with their jobs, mostly in different directions, it made it difficult for either of them to make the relationship stronger than it already was.

It had been more than six weeks since Rachel had heard from Jamie, so she wanted to make the occasion special by reserving a table at the Grimsdyke Hotel. This beautiful old house was the last home of W.S. Gilbert, the librettist of the Gilbert & Sullivan duo, who had died in the arms of two young women, next to the swimming pool. The pool had now been filled in and a garden had been created there and dedicated to Gilbert's memory. This was one of Jamie's favourite restaurants. The food was excellent and was complemented by the amusing excerpts from the operettas, sung by the waiters and waitresses as they moved about their duties.

Rachel busied herself selecting her outfit for the evening and then went to take a shower. She had to appear very sleek and businesslike during the week but when she had the opportunity to relax she chose a completely feminine look and tonight she wanted to be 'all woman'. She removed her clothes and took a long look at herself in the full-length mirror behind the bathroom door. She turned to see if there were any blemishes, and lifted her long, dark hair away from her neck.

Normally she wore her hair in a long plait, wound around her head to add extra height. Rachel was very conscious of being five foot four tall and she felt that she needed to add inches by wearing high-heels and tailored clothes. Tonight she would wear her highest heels, with her hair down and her new red, designer dress to complement her olive skin and dark brown eyes.

The steam in the bathroom was misting the mirror now and Rachel wasted no further time. After her shower she dressed carefully and, as a final touch, added a pair of diamond earrings.

Jamie had presented them to her as a birthday gift when he returned from a trip to Europe. He had been to Amsterdam on business and during one of the luncheons had met a diamond merchant who invited him to his showrooms and introduced him to his top designer. It had given Jamie enormous pleasure and satisfaction to choose the stones and then consult with the designer as to how they would be set. The earrings had to be unique, he had explained: they were intended for a very special person. The result had been a pair of delicate lover's knots in 18 carat gold, encrusted with sparkling diamonds – quite exquisite.

It was now 7.30 pm and time to go, the diamonds glittered with fire as Rachel gathered her coat and handbag just as the doorbell sounded. Jamie had arrived and she did not want to keep him waiting.

They both thoroughly enjoyed the evening, and it allowed Jamie some relief and respite from all that had happened during the last week. The playful, frivolous lyrics of Gilbert's songs was a sparkling counterpoint to their gentle conversation, relaxing his mind, and his body was content with the satisfaction of an excellent meal. When they arrived at Rachel's home she made two glasses of mint tea to help digest the meal, then poured a glass of brandy for Jamie and a Cointreau for herself. As Jamie sipped his drink, Rachel enquired about his trip to Ireland and his request for her help.

As Jamie recounted his story, Rachel was plainly astonished, and curious to see the watch. Jamie dug into his overnight bag, pulled out the red case and passed it over to her. She stared with evident distaste at the faded gold swastika, but when she opened the case, her expression changed to one of horror.

With one finger and thumb she lifted the watch with the heavy chain hanging from it, as if extracting an overgrown spider from its web, laid it on the coffee table in front of her and asked him to open it for her as she could not bring herself to touch it again. The thought of Hitler, that excuse for a human being, handling the watch made her shudder.

After a full examination of the watch and all it contained, she asked what help he thought she could offer.

'I was hoping you might be able to suggest someone you might know – a Jew, I mean – who might like to have it.'

'I don't believe that a Jew or any decent person would want anything to do with that watch.'

'I agree, Rachel.' Jamie replied, 'but my father made it clear that he had promised he'd sell it back to Manny Rosenberg – or at the very least he'd make sure that it should pass into the hands of a Jew.'

'I don't know anyone who would want it, or anyone who would understand why Manny wanted it, but perhaps my grandfather may have some ideas. He is about the same age as Manny, and experienced the same difficulties during the war. Tomorrow I will call him – perhaps we could visit him in London ...' She paused. 'But stop worrying about it now, I have something else in mind for you tonight. Finish your drink, my love and come with me!'

* * *

The next morning Jamie was on his way back to east London in Rachel's car to meet her grandfather. They entered Aldgate and passed Bloom's 'World Famous Kosher Restaurant', and Gardner's Corner.

Nothing seemed to change very much around here, Jamie thought. Stepney East Station was now called Docklands but otherwise remained the same.

They drove through Commercial Road and then right into Limehouse and Beccles Street then Trinidad Street. Jamie was now completely lost in the narrow streets leading to Poplar. They crossed Westferry Road into Garford then on to Ming Street and Poplar High Street.

'I come this way to avoid the heavy traffic on East India Dock Road,' Rachel explained as the car finally came to a stop in Cottage Street.

Jamie was introduced to Aaron Kossoff, Rachel's grandfather, who made them very welcome. He had lived in the East End since the war, having managed to escape from Germany in the late 1930s, when life had become not just difficult but intolerable for Jewish people. Now in his early nineties, he still had a very good memory and the stories he told of his experiences were extraordinary.

Rachel waited for a suitable moment between his reminiscences to tell him why they had come to see him. After explaining the background of the watch and its description, she was about to remove the watch from her handbag when the old man raised his hand.

'Please Rachel, I do not want to see this dreadful watch, keep it in your handbag. The information you seek to satisfy Jamie's promise to his father may be found by contacting the Simon Wiesenthal Centre in Vienna. Wiesenthal has spent a lifetime searching out those Nazi monsters, who hid themselves away after the war like rats. He has found most of them and watched as they were finally brought to justice.'

* * *

They returned to Rachel's house and rang the Centre.

Rachel took some time explaining in detail the reason for her call to satisfy the woman who answered. They could overhear the lady explaining the information Rachel had given her to someone, who did not seem at all interested.

'All my time is spent searching for Nazi criminals, I have no time to consider the inheritance of Hitler's pocket watch. He is dead anyway. Tell them to throw the watch away and leave me alone.'

The woman apologised, saying that Mr Wiesenthal could not help and would not come to the phone.

'So that's it,' said Rachel.

'I don't think so,' replied Jamie. 'I have just been assigned by my company to visit our hotels in Vienna and carry out a new marketing structure for them. It will give me the opportunity to pester Wiesenthal until I get some idea on how I can complete the promise to my father.'

3   Vienna

THE FOUR-STAR Hilton Vienna Danube stood on the Handelski and was one of six Hilton hotels in Vienna. They had been informed of Jamie's intended visit, which had made the necessary introductions easy and less time-wasting. As Jamie left for the company suite overlooking the Danube, which had been reserved for him, he turned to the concierge and asked him to find the address of Simon Wiesenthal for him.

'Is that Wiesenthal, the Nazi hunter, sir?' the young man enquired.

'Yes, Simon Wiesenthal – I need his help,' Jamie replied and left the reception for his room.

The concierge looked clearly confused, wondering how a Nazi hunter was going to help with the new marketing strategy.

Jamie had only just started to unpack his suitcase when there was a knock on the door.

'Yes?'

'It's the concierge, sir.'

Jamie opened the door to find the young man standing there with an envelope on a silver tray. 'Your information, sir.'

Jamie took the envelope, briefly looked at the address and passed a tip to the concierge, knowing that this young man could be very useful for further information.

'Do you intend visiting Mr Wiesenthal, sir?'

'Yes, I do. Why do you ask?'

'I believe he is a very difficult man to see unless you have good information about Nazis. If you do not have such information, the only way to meet him would be casually, by a visit to the Café Peluso on Meiereistrabe. Mr Wiesenthal usually takes a lemon tea and bagel most mornings, about 11 am, except Sundays, sir.'

Jamie thanked the young man and offered him another, more generous, tip.

* * *

At eleven the next morning, Simon Wiesenthal was sitting in the café, just as the concierge had said, with a glass of lemon tea and a half-eaten bagel.

Jamie had never seen or met him before, but had no doubts as to who he was. The adjacent table was free with a vacant chair backing onto the chair the man was sitting in, so as Jamie sat down he made a point of banging his chair back, just as Wiesenthal was sipping his tea.

'Oh, I am very sorry, *mein herr*,' Jamie exclaimed.

'Don't worry about it, young man,' Wiesenthal replied. 'They put these chairs too close together, trying to squeeze more customers into their café.' He looked more closely at Jamie as he sat down. 'Are you here on holiday?'

'Not exactly,' Jamie replied carefully. 'I work for the Hilton Hotel Group as their marketing director – I am here to complete a new marketing strategy for them and hopefully fulfil a deathbed promise I made to my father.'

Wiesenthal put down his cup. 'A promise to a dying man? That is really something of a commitment. I wish you luck to fulfil it as quickly as you can.'

'Maybe you can help me with this promise if I explain to you what it is?'

'If it involves Vienna or Austria, perhaps I can but otherwise I do not think so,' said Wiesenthal, shrugging his shoulders.

Jamie went on to explain about his father's gold watch, being careful not to reveal too much about its origin and details. It was, he said, his father's wish to return the watch to an old Jewish pawnbroker, who had kindly accepted the watch as a pledge for many years when his father was short of cash; in appreciation for the pawnbroker's kindness he wanted him to have it.

'If it was not possible to give it to him,' Jamie explained, 'then my father said I should find another Jew who would accept it as a gift—'

'A moment, young man,' Wiesenthal broke in. 'A watch, you say ? Of this I have heard before. A woman telephoned my home the other day. I repeat what I advised then – throw the watch away ... It will bring you nothing but grief.'

'But I must complete my promise.'

'I do not see any problem with keeping your father's wish. What are you finding so difficult?' Wiesenthal asked.

'Well, unfortunately the old pawnbroker died before I could pass the watch over to him, so I am therefore left to find a Jew to accept the watch as a gift.'

'Is this watch valuable?'

'It is solid 18 carat gold with a chain and fob,' Jamie replied.

'Can I see this watch? Do you have it with you?'

'As a matter of fact, I do have the watch with me. Perhaps I could pass it on to *you*?'

'You could, but I may not be the "suitable Jew" your old pawnbroker would have wished to have the watch!'

Jamie carefully removed the watch case from his pocket and placed it on the table in front of Wiesenthal, upside down to hide the swastika on the front.

Simon Wiesenthal lifted the case with the thumb and forefinger of each hand at its sides as he turned it over to reveal the Nazi sign.

Upon seeing the swastika on top of the case he dropped it back onto the table, taking a large gasp of breath at the same time and placing his left hand over his mouth.

There was complete silence for several minutes as Jamie watched Wiesenthal's eyes widen as he looked at the red case in front of him. Many thoughts seemed to be rushing through the Austrian's mind, as he contemplated the container, and whether he should open it or not.

Finally he slid the case back to Jamie, saying, 'I will have nothing to do with this watch.'

'I am only asking for some advice sir, that's all, nothing else.'

'Let me see the watch then, but you open the case and show it to me. I do not want to touch it.'

Jamie turned the case towards himself, so that when the lid flew open. Wiesenthal could not see the contents. He then lifted the watch by the chain with the watch face looking towards the man opposite.

He then turned the watch around and saw the look of horror on Wiesenthal's face at seeing Hitler's head engraved on the back.

Jamie opened the back to reveal the inscription.

'This watch is poison,' said Wiesenthal, 'and it will eventually kill you, I am sure of that fact.'

'What are you saying, Mr Wiesenthal? Why is it dangerous and how can it harm me?'

'Tell me,' Wiesenthal asked, 'how did the old pawnbroker die?'

'He was murdered during a robbery at his shop.'

'And what did they steal that was so valuable to murder a man for?'

'Only the pledge book was missing according to the police.'

'How did your father die?'

'From a heart attack at a family celebration,' Jamie reluctantly replied. 'He had a weak heart, which had been the case for many years and he would not take the doctor's advice to stop smoking and drinking.'

'Did your father ever have anyone call on him asking after this watch?'

'Not as far as I know. But his flat had been burgled recently.'

'What did they steal?'

'I couldn't find anything of value missing. Just a lot of mess, as though they were searching for something.'

'Is this watch genuine, or is it a faked copy?'

'That, I simply do not know,' Jamie admitted.

'Well, I suggest that the first thing you do is to get it checked out by a reputable auction house. If it turns out to be the real thing, I must warn you that your life is in serious danger. Even if you are able to pass it on, you will still be in grave danger of being tortured and murdered for the whereabouts of the watch. The same situation will arise if you destroy the watch. Either way I do not see how you can fulfil your father's dying wish and survive.'

With that, Wiesenthal clasped Jamie by the hand and strode away.

The walk back to the hotel was not far, but it gave Jamie an opportunity to reflect on the conversation he had just experienced. He could not believe that there were neo-Nazis who would commit the atrocities the old man had spoken of and murder for a pocket watch. Wiesenthal was so involved in the past that he saw the past and present as one, but he had been so convincing that Jamie started to feel that he was being followed, so much so that he even stopped on a couple of occasions to look over his shoulder, only to find there was no one there.

The work he was to carry out for the six hotels did not take more than three days with the assistance of the managers of the hotels concerned and the local Director of Tourism for Vienna.

Once the new marketing strategy had been passed to head office for approval by the board of directors, he would have to wait for their decision or the recommended modifications that had been received.

Jamie sat at the dressing table of his hotel room and wondered what he might do with himself for the next few days while awaiting a reply from head office. As he sat contemplating what to do in this beautiful and interesting city, he found his hand playing with the chain and fob of the pocket watch.

When he realised what he was doing he took a closer look at the fob. Facing him was the outstretched eagle with the swastika at its feet. He turned it over and found the Eagle's Nest Fortress engraved on the other side. Until now Jamie had thought nothing of this place, and never considered visiting the area.

He telephoned reception and asked for the concierge to visit his room.

'What do you know of the Eagle's Nest at Berchtesgaden?' he asked.

The concierge looked pleased. It was obviously something he knew about – and another opportunity for him to be given a tip. 'Only that it was built in 1940 under the supervision of

Martin Bormann as a gift from the Nazi Party to Adolf Hitler for his fiftieth birthday. It was never used as a fortress, and Adolf Hitler never lived there – he only used it to entertain visitors. After the war the Americans wanted to pull it down, but were persuaded otherwise by the local residents. So it is now a tourist attraction with stunning views over Austria's mountain ranges.' he replied.

'Can you tell me any more?'

'Well, sir, Hitler did live in Berchtesgaden, but his home has been pulled down, along with the others of top Nazi leaders who lived there during the war. To visit the Eagle's Nest you will have to go to the small village of Obersalzberg, where they have tourist buses that take visitors to the fortress.'

'How far is it from Vienna?'

'Approximately 186 kilometres, or a little less on the motorway, which is a waste in my opinion because you would miss out on the wonderful views on the scenic route.'

'Does it take very long to get there in a car?'

'About two and a half hours on the scenic route and a little less on the motorway. I can get a car for you, if you wish, Mr O'Byrne .'

'Yes. Tomorrow would suit me nicely. Please arrange it for me and thank you for all your information,' said Jamie, as yet another tip changed hands.

4   The Eagle's Nest

HE NEXT MORNING a silver Grey Porsche 928 sports car was awaiting Jamie at the front of the hotel, thanks to contacts of the concierge. It was a truly beautiful drive to Berchtesgaden on such a lovely morning, the two and a half hours passed very quickly. The view of the Eagle's Nest, high on the pinnacle of the mountain, as he entered the village of Obersalzberg, was unmistakable.

Jamie parked in the town to seek out the Tourist Information Office and avoid wasting time by not missing anything he might have wanted to see. The young girl behind the counter seemed more like a university student working her half term than a tourist information guide, but she was very knowledgeable and helpful. Jamie was directed to take the tour bus to the Eagle's Nest as cars are no longer permitted to take the dangerous winding track up the mountain.

There were several buses doing this tourist route. They were easily identified by the beautiful paintings of the Eagle's Nest and mountains on their sides.

The bus Jamie entered was filled in no time and as they started up the mountain he could see why casual motorists were not allowed on this virtually single winding road. The cars coming down the track would be travelling so fast that there would be hardly any room to allow the car going up to pass. Many accidents had occurred on this road before unauthorised traffic was banned.

At the coach car park it was necessary to pass through a tunnel. This was lined with marble and about three hundred metres long, leading to a reception area. Here an elevator was waiting to take visitors the final three hundred metres up into the Fortress.

Jamie was very impressed with this old lift. It was built in 1940 and was still able to carry 53 passengers at a time. The interior of the lift was covered with highly polished brass and there was a round Venetian mirror facing the doors. This, Jamie thought, was where Hitler would have checked his appearance as he entered the lift. Around the inside were bench seats covered in emerald green leather.

The Eagle's Nest was rather less elaborate than the lift. It was indeed like a fortress, simply constructed of bare solid breezeblock, with flags and paintings on the walls.

A closer examination of the interior revealed several rooms where Hitler entertained his guests, with many large paintings and pictures on the walls depicting these events. A huge fireplace in one room was a gift from Mussolini.

From the balcony the views were spectacular. It was a beautiful clear day and the mountain ranges that seemed to encircle this fortress could be seen very clearly. The area was packed with tourists from all over the world.

Before leaving, Jamie visited the cafeteria. The basic menu of Austrian fare didn't appeal to him, so he ordered a lager. But when he reached into his pocket to pay the bill, he discovered to his dismay that his wallet was missing. He paid with loose change in his inside pocket.

This was not a place that pickpockets frequented, he thought, as he returned to the bus. Fortunately, he had his return bus ticket with him and a credit card to tide him over.

On his arrival back in Berchtesgaden he made his way to the local police station, where he made a report of the theft. The policeman sitting at a typewriter, insisted on knowing everything about the wallet in detail, including the colour, size and contents. The policeman tapped away on his keyboard as Jamie passed on the information, and finally asked him to read and confirm that what he had written was correct.

Jamie signed the form and passed it back to the policeman who returned a few minutes later with a clear plastic envelope which contained what looked like his wallet. It was removed from the plastic envelope and placed in front of Jamie alongside the report form.

'Is this your wallet?'

Jamie examined the item and contents to find that there was nothing missing at all.

'Yes this is it,' he confirmed with a sigh of relief.

He was asked to sign another form before being allowed to keep the wallet.

'This wallet was handed in not more than half an hour ago,' the policeman informed him.

'Where was it found?'

'At the Gasthof Waldluft café.'

'That's incredible!' Jamie exclaimed. 'I have never visited that café. Did the person who handed it in leave an address or telephone number for me to thank and reward them?'

'No,' the policeman replied, 'the woman just left the wallet and informed us where it was found and then left.'

Jamie thanked him, puzzled and confused but pleased to have retrieved it.

On his arrival back at the hotel he went straight to his room and checked the wallet once again. Inside he found a plain white business card with nothing more than a telephone number, in gold letters.

On the bottom right of the card was written:

Call Me

This must be the person that found my wallet, thought Jamie. He lifted the hotel room telephone and punched in the prefix number to make an external call, then listened to the dialling tone and wondered who would answer the call, and how he would introduce himself.

'Good Evening Mr O'Byrne.' It was a woman's voice. 'I was hoping you would accept my invitation to call me.'

The woman avoided any discussion about the loss of his wallet; she seemed more interested in meeting Jamie for a drink in the cocktail bar of the hotel where he was staying. He had no reason not to meet this woman who had apparently found his wallet at a café he had never visited and then presented it to the police station. So he agreed to their meeting in the cocktail bar – at least he would not have to search around Vienna to find another venue for their meeting.

As Jamie entered the cocktail bar a lady dressed in black beckoned him to a quiet corner of the bar. She was strikingly attractive, in her early thirties, expensively dressed in clothes that had been tailor-made for her and revealed every curve of her perfect body. Her make-up had been carefully applied, and her shoulder-length black hair shone like silk from the dim lights of the bar.

'What would you like to drink, Jamie?' she asked in an indifferent manner. 'What are you drinking?' he replied, thinking that this would be a polite reply to a lady he had only just met.

'A White Lady,' was her confident reply.

She did not offer her name, and took control of the conversation after ordering Jamie's cocktail. She asked him about his visit to Vienna and Berchtesgaden and he explained about his marketing work for Hilton Hotels.

'Why did you want me to call you?' he asked.

'You have something we want. We will give you a very large sum of money for it.'

'I think you have the wrong person,' Jamie replied. 'I do not have anything here in Vienna, or in London, that could be worth a large amount of money.'

'Perhaps you do not appreciate its value as yet. Maybe you think that no one is interested in it.'

'Now you have awakened my curiosity, please tell me what is this item of value I am not aware of.'

'It is your father's watch. We know he died in Ireland and as you are the only son it is natural that he would have passed it on to you.'

When Jamie heard her mention the watch, a chill of fear ran down his spine: this situation seemed to be going in the direction that Wiesenthal had predicted.

'My father's watch,' Jamie replied, with a look of surprise on his face. 'Why on earth would anyone be interested in an old Ingersol army watch. He never gave it to me and as far as I know it was buried with him or perhaps the undertaker is now wearing it.'

'That is not the watch I was referring to,' she answered sharply. She had now dropped any pretence of pleasantries. Her pale blue eyes gazed at him, menacingly. 'It is the pocket watch your father had that we are interested in.'

'I know nothing of any pocket watch. But if you tell me more about the one you believe my father had, then maybe I could get the family to search for you.'

'That will not be necessary, Mr O'Byrne. We know where the watch is. It will only be a matter of time, money or otherwise before it will be back with us, the rightful owners. Back where it belongs.'

She then stood, picked up her large black leather handbag and left the hotel; leaving Jamie to pick up the drinks bill.

* * *

As he entered his room he felt that someone, other then the chambermaid, had paid it a visit in his absence. After a careful search of every part of the room, including drawers, wardrobe and bathroom, everything seemed just as he had left it but he still felt sure that someone had been there.

As he sat on the king-size bed, looking around the room, his business briefcase came into view. He immediately made a grab for the case and inspected the codes on the two combination locks. As a security caution he always left his case locked with the numbers 1212 in place; if his case had been opened the numbers would have been different. He took a close look at the numbers and realised that they were different. The case had been opened, although when he inspected the contents they were just as he had left them.

It now occurred to him that it had been a good idea to seal the watch in a plain brown envelope and pass it to the concierge to deposit in the hotel safe.

Fear was starting to affect Jamie, a cold sweat breaking out on his forehead.

This watch and my father's dying wish may well cost me my life, he thought.

He decided there and then to have the watch forwarded to the London Head Office via the internal mail system. When the watch was in his keeping, his life was not safe and he needed time to think the situation through without worrying about the watch.

41

5   𝕿ime for 𝕿hought

AFTER JAMIE collected his suitcase from the airport conveyor belt at Heathrow Airport, he made for the nearest public telephone to call Rachel. She was delighted to hear that he was back home and curious to learn how his meeting with Wiesenthal had gone, plus any new information he had obtained about the watch.

As soon as she heard Jamie's car in the drive, she went to the door to welcome him home. Once Jamie had taken a shower and changed into some clothes that he always kept at Rachel's place, he settled down with an aperitif of Royal Kir that she had prepared for him from the half bottle of Moet & Chandon champagne and cassis.

'Mmmm ... gorgeous. What's the plan for this evening, Rachel?'

'I thought we would eat at home rather than going out to a restaurant. I want to know everything that happened in Vienna, without the distraction and interruptions of a restaurant,' replied Rachel, as she pottered about her spacious kitchen. She had prepared Beef Wellington as the main course, with a starter of chicken liver pâté; for desert she would surprise him with a delicious Black Forest Gateau topped with fresh cream.

It was not until they had finished the main course and a bottle of Nuit St George red wine that Jamie started to speak of his experience in Vienna. He had let Rachel lead the conversation during the starter and main course, and now that she was relaxed he could unfold his story.

He recounted his interview with Simon Wiesenthal and the incident of losing his wallet at the Eagle's Nest and then finding it again. When he mentioned the 'woman in black', who had informed him that they would obtain the watch – one way or another, Rachel gasped with surprise. About to place the last of her gateau into her mouth, she missed completely and watched helplessly as her dessert fell onto her plate with a plop.

'This is terrible, Jamie. It sounds very dangerous to me. Who do you think these people are?'

'Probably neo-Nazis who want to obtain as much genuine Nazi regalia as possible, to justify their movement and support their historical background.'

'Do you really think that they would stop at nothing to get their hands on this watch?'

'I really do not know, but bearing in mind Wiesenthal's warning, I have taken the precaution of placing it outside of my possession. Please don't ask me where it is: the less anyone else knows, the safer it will be – for all of us.'

'Oh, Jamie,' whispered Rachel. 'Please be careful.'

The next day Jamie drove to his Chelsea house to find that, like his father's flat, it too had been totally ransacked. The leather Chesterfield couch and chairs had been slashed and their stuffing strewn over the Chinese carpets. The same treatment had been given to the bedroom with the mattress and pillows shredded into pieces; the whole place was a mess. As Jamie inspected the damage he realised that this was not just a detailed search for the pocket watch. It was meant as a warning, to show the extent these people were prepared to go to in order to have the watch passed over to them.

He left the apartment and drove back to Rachel's house to discuss his dilemma and hopefully come to a conclusion on what he should do next. Rachel was always a very good sounding-board when he had problems to sort out. She would analyse each aspect and put a variety of options together for consideration, leaving Jamie to make the final decision, with her encouragement. This had always proved successful in the past and he hoped that it would be so on this occasion.

Rachel was delighted to see him return and immediately made him welcome. She listened intently as he recounted the most recent events at his home.

'This is getting very serious, Jamie. We must consider a course of action to protect you from any further danger.'

He explained that he had not yet informed the police of the damage to his house and Rachel was in agreement with his decision.

'Let's consider some alternatives before going down that road,' said Jamie.

After two long hours of discussion and several pots of coffee, it was concluded that the favoured option, at this point in time, would be for him to disappear from the clutches of these people and 'lie low' for a few weeks. This would give Jamie more time to think the situation through and maybe, just maybe, the villains would have another project on their plate to follow up, giving Jamie time to dispose of the watch in a way that he felt his father would have approved.

It was finally decided to send Jamie away on an extended holiday, to a place far away from Europe. Rachel was not known to these neo-Nazis and it was agreed that she would make the reservation and pay for the trip in her own name; to this end she left Jamie at her house and made her way into the city.

Kuoni Travel Agents were a company she has used before, so making her way from Knightsbridge Underground Station, along Brompton Road to Montpelier Street, was quite familiar.

She had no idea where she was going to send Jamie and hoped the young travel assistant, sitting opposite her, would have some ideas. They scanned through pages of brochures of Japan, China, Vietnam, Hong Kong and Malaysia, when Rachel noticed a special 'two for the price of one' offer in the Seychelle Islands.

'That's it, that's perfect,' she said, especially as the holiday was due to start the following afternoon.

When she informed Jamie of her holiday hideaway he was delighted. She had booked a taxi for the morning and obtained loads of information about the Indian Ocean Islands at the travel agents. They would read this on the thirteen-hour flight as the plane had only one short stop off, for refuelling, in Nairobi.

6   𝔗𝔥𝔢 𝔖𝔢𝔶𝔠𝔥𝔢𝔩𝔩𝔢𝔰

HE CAPITAL of the main island of Mahé is Victoria, which features the smallest statue of Queen Victoria, in the centre of the city. The whole island is only eighteen miles in length and five miles wide, but delightfully green and welcoming.

Rachel and Jamie were booked into the five-star Fisherman's Cove Hotel, in the luxury Allamanda Suite. The hotel was only thirty minutes from the airport in the Beau Vallon Bay and had 68 rooms. The pictures of the restaurant and cocktail bar, overlooking the bay, looked very inviting. When the flight finally touched down at the Seychelles Airport the first thing that struck them, as they crossed the airstrip, was the heat and humidity, and they couldn't wait for a shower and a cooling drink.

The Kuoni courier was waiting for them. She introduced herself and directed them to the Kuoni coach as their suitcases were taken and deposited in the luggage compartment. Jamie carefully observed the other twenty couples who were joining them on the coach, to satisfy himself that the 'Woman in Black' wasn't one of them. The thirty-minute coach trip to the hotel took them over the 900 metre high mountain that dominates the centre of the island. It was very pleasant after the long flight. The huge palm trees, flora and fauna were beautiful and the Indian Ocean was a calm, turquoise blue.

* * *

On arrival at the hotel their suitcases were removed from the coach and deposited in their suite for them. They were introduced to the hotel manager at the reception desk, who explained that this was a small hotel that operated on a personal basis to their guests. They would be left free to enjoy their stay in seclusion in their hotel suite and beach or they could join the rest of the guests in the restaurant, lounge and cocktail bar; the choice was theirs alone.

The Allamanda suite was just as they had expected from the travel agents brochure. The pretty little chambermaid was waiting to show them around the suite and demonstrate how everything operated; from the hotel telephone they could contact her, at any time, for room service via the reception desk. Before leaving she offered to assist Rachel with unpacking the suitcases, Rachel declined, however, as she preferred to do it herself. Jamie gave the girl a tip as she left and started to explore the suite, balcony and beach, giving consideration to their security: as Rachel had involved herself in his dilemma, she was now in as much danger as himself.

For the first three days and nights they confined themselves to their suite, using the room service for all their meals. They could walk directly from the suite onto their secluded beach for a swim in the warm, salty water of the Indian Ocean. Rachel had obtained some further information about the favoured tourist sites and, with the help of the chambermaid, had planned a tour of the island for them. Jamie studied the planned routes and beauty spots before calling the reception to hire a car for the next day.

At 9 am they were awoken by the phone. It was the receptionist informing Jamie that the hire car was waiting for him at the hotel entrance. After breakfast on the balcony of their suite, Rachel gathered everything they would need for the day's tour including binoculars, cameras, swimwear and snorkels, towels and sun lotion. The chambermaid informed them that they could collect their packed lunch boxes from the reception desk as they left.

Jamie was a little shocked to see that the hire car was a Mini Moke. He had not specified the type or model of car he preferred and the vehicle came as quite a change from the luxury XJ12 Double Six company car he drove at home. He made his way to the reception desk to enquire if it was possible to hire a normal car for the day, rather than the basic runabout.

'Yes, of course,' the receptionist replied, 'but we have found that our guests are not very impressed with the standard hire cars; they often have large dents on the roof and bonnet from falling coconuts. The Mini Mokes are more suited to our roads and with the open top you can enjoy the fresh air and sunshine.'

With Rachel's encouragement Jamie agreed to accept the car for the days excursion and the picnic lunch boxes and other requirements for the day were deposited between the front and back seats. Jamie accidentally crunched the gears as they shot out of the hotel entrance but wrestling with the gears and bouncing over the bumps were all part of the fun. Rachel started giggling when Jamie hit a pothole and nearly fell out of the Moke and slowly their mood lightened and they began to enjoy themselves.

On their way to Victoria they wandered through the small narrow streets, getting a feel for the Seychellois people and their way of life. Jamie commented on how attractive the girls were and their lovely figures, hiding behind the colourful, simple dresses they wore. Their chambermaid had recommended that they visit the church and clock tower, and also the souvenir shops because the souvenirs were locally produced. These included a variety of seashells, some of which were very large while others were so tiny that they were made into bracelets and necklaces; there were huge turtle shells which had been polished and cut into picture frames etc. and there was also the Coco de Mare, a unique twinned coconut with a remarkable resemblance to a lady's bottom. Jamie picked up one of these in the shop and asked Rachel to turn her back to him so that he could make a comparison!

After purchasing a few souvenirs they made their way to the Rendezvous Restaurant for coffee before setting off for the Sans Souci road to take them over the hills onto the mountain tracks where it was much cooler and less humid than the city. The Mini Moke suited these rough mountain roads very well but the vehicle was not at all comfortable as Jamie, yet again, crunched through the gears of the car which appeared to have no form of suspension at all. They bounced along and it was a relief for them both when they reached the old Mission Lodge, which offered spectacular views over the coast of Mahé. Rachel informed Jamie that apparently the Mission Lodge was built on the ruins of the ancient school for slave children, which gave the impression that the landowners were not opposed to educating their slave workers, unlike other countries at that time, who did not allow this by law.

While Jamie was taking pictures, Rachel was using the binoculars and pointing out scenic views for him to photograph. She was also enjoying the wonderful colours of the birdlife in the area, particularly a rose-red parakeet on a tree nearby. It was so close to her that she could see the beautiful colours of green and rose red at the nape of its neck and his beak. It was wonderful to observe so much natural life all around them; normally they would only see such things in a zoo. A tiny green tree frog wanted to get to know Rachel as she spotted him on her shoe; she watched him crawl up her bare leg and when she placed her hand, very slowly, on her leg the little fellow climbed onto the back of it. She was able to lift him close to her face where she could inspect him .He seemed as interested in her as she was in him and she called softly to Jamie to come over and look at this tiny animal.

'Fantastic!' Jamie exclaimed, 'but I would need a macro lens on my SLR camera to take a picture of that. I got a good one though of the spider, on the web in the tree, above your head.'

He laughed at Rachel's reaction when she looked up and saw an enormous spider. It must have measured at least eight inches across from the tip of one leg to the tip of the other. The body was huge, covered in black fluffy fur with yellow rings around both body and legs.

'Is it poisonous?' she asked.

'I have no idea,' he replied, as Rachel backed away from her position underneath the awesome spider ... the tree frog had disappeared!

They continued their tour to the tea plantation for some refreshing tea and pastries, while they enjoyed the beautiful landscape laid out before them. Jamie decided to stop at Grande Anse beach for their picnic lunch. The sand was soft and golden and the water a beautiful blue and clear enough to see the seabed and the small fish that scattered away as they paddled along the shore. The hotel had included some wine with the picnic and after they had eaten they swam and played like children in the warm, silky water.

Rachel looked so lovely with her long dark hair, wet and shining from the reflection of the sun on the water. She was wearing a white bikini which was becoming transparent in the sea so that Jamie could see her dark nipples through the bikini top, which had hardened in the water and pushed against the material. There was no-one else on the beach as Jamie and Rachel wrestled playfully on the foreshore, rolling in and out of the waves.

Finally she lay back on the sand with her hair spread out around her head and Jamie gathered her into his arms, kissing her passionately, hard and firm as the water flowed around and between them. Gently he removed the restraining top and gazed with excitement at her beautiful breasts: they never failed to excite his passion for her; he lowered his head to her breast and softly licked her nipples. The thrill of feeling his touch made Rachel quiver and when Jamie entered her it was the most satisfying sensation. The waves sucked the sand from beneath them but they were lost in each other. Jamie sensed when she was ready to climax and slowed his rhythm, talking to her and stroking her until her limbs trembled and she could wait no longer.

'Now my love ... now.'

All her passionate energy flowed from her as she cried out weakly with a gently moan of satisfaction. Jamie relaxed and they lay on the beach while the warm waves lapped at their toes.

The sun dried them and they rose to dress, lazy and languid, totally relaxed and perfectly at ease with each other. Time now to continue their journey around the island.

* * *

By the time they arrived back at the hotel it was late and the roads were pitch black without street lighting; it seemed as if there was very little, if any, twilight time in the Seychelles. The chambermaid had left a light supper in the room for them and a bottle of French Chablis in the refrigerator. The pleasure of the day's travel, together with the fresh air and exercise, sent them both into a deep sleep and it was late by the time they awoke the next morning. The maid had brought their breakfast but left without disturbing them .

They showered together in the large wet room. Rachel loved to shower with Jamie, feeling his large, gentle hands on her back and rubbing the natural sponge over her body. It was inevitable that they made love again before their day began.

They ate breakfast on the balcony in their shower robes and talked of the enjoyment of the previous day's travel. While they were speaking Jamie looked out across the ocean at the various yachts, some at anchor while others were sailing off to discover the secrets of other small islands. There were such a variety of yachts to be seen that he left the breakfast table to fetch his binoculars so he could watch their shapes more closely and explained to Rachel what they were. From huge schooners and sloops down to ketch rigged and Bermuda yachts and catamarans.

Jamie remembered the times when he went fishing with his father in Ireland during his school holidays. The thrill of letting go the warps that tied them to the harbour wall and as soon as the sails were up and the auxiliary engine switched off, they were carried off with the wind. His father would say, 'Free at last, Jamie. Just you and me, the freedom of the wind and nature. No Garda, no traffic or regulations. Only our own rules which we impose for the safety of our vessel ...'

Wonderful memories.

7 Ocean Dream

ACHEL'S SUGGESTION of getting away had proved to be the right one as Jamie' confidence had started to return and the events surrounding his fathers pocket watch receded.

'Let's charter a yacht,' he suggested.

'Why not,' she replied. She had every confidence in his ability to sail most yachts and was as keen as he to explore some of the tiny atolls that formed the Seychelle islands.

The only yacht available for them to charter for a week was the Swan 32, a Bermuda rigged yacht, 32 feet long and very well appointed for most sea conditions. It was a strong vessel and Jamie knew its characteristics very well. Before committing himself to chartering this yacht and parting with any money, he insisted on checking its condition and safety equipment, all of which he found satisfactory.

Finally he checked the sea cocks, opening and closing them to ensure they had not seized up or corroded with the salt sea water and that there were sufficient wooden bungs to block them if they started to leak. He even operated the sea toilet to make sure it functioned properly.

It was a fine-looking yacht called *Ocean Dream* and Jamie was now satisfied to sail her anywhere. He wanted to take Rachel on the first day of their week's charter, for what he called a shakedown sail, to give both of them an opportunity to get a feel for the yacht and using all the sails to see how it responded to the various points of sail.

Ocean Dream was at anchor and with the help of the owner they had filled the galley and fridge with all the essentials of food and wine, that they would need for their cruise. They said farewell to the owner as he left in an inflatable dingy and Jamie wasted no time in switching on the Volvo Penta engine, which quickly kicked into life. He released the main sail sheets and started to raise the main sail by pulling on the halyard, after releasing the sail ties that secured the sail to the boom which was now flagging from side to side. He reminded Rachel to be careful of the boom while this process was going on. 'It can give you a nasty crack on the head while you're standing in the cockpit.'

Once the main sail was fully raised he secured the halyard to the jamming cleat on the mast and joined Rachel in the cockpit. He asked her to take control of the tiller while he unfurled the Genoa sail and told her to keep the head of the yacht into the wind. The sails were now flapping loosely in the wind and Jamie explained that he was going forward to raise the anchor and that she should watch what he was doing because when he raised his hand above his head, the signal would mean that the anchor was raised and they were ready to sail off.

The anchor was raised with the assistance of an electric windlass and once it was secured on board Jamie returned to the cockpit, securing the main sail sheets into the jamming cleats and coiling the Genoa sheet around the jamming winch, which he tightened with the aid of the winch handle. *Ocean Dream* now heeled gently to the port side as she pointed, close hauled, into the wind.

Sitting on the starboard cockpit side and holding the tiller towards her, Rachel was keeping the yacht on a steady course, exclaiming to Jamie that he had set the sails so well that the yacht was almost sailing herself, with hardly any effort on the tiller. The gentle wind force of 4 to 5 filled the sails of *Ocean Dream* as she cut her way through the calm waters of the Indian Ocean without the sound of the diesel engine. Jamie took a deep breath as he remembered his father's words at this stage of every voyage, when they were leaving the shore behind them and making their way towards the horizon: ''Twas like leaving all their troubles behind them ...'

On this occasion it was the anxiety concerning his father's watch that faded into the distance. He had almost forgotten that this was to be a shake-down cruise, to try out all the equipment on board before committing themselves to a distant shore. Fortunately however, he had no reason to concern himself as everything functioned perfectly.

The course was set for Silbouette, the third largest island, and Jamie found some fishing tackle in one of the cockpit lockers and thought it might be an idea to toss it over the stern of the yacht to try a little fishing. It was not long before he saw a fish, attached to his line, bouncing out of the water. It was a bonito of about three kilos,

'We can barbecue that on the beach this evening,' he told Rachel.

Within a relatively short time they had arrived and spying a suitable anchorage, Jamie secured the boat, pointing her head to the wind and leaving out enough chain for the depth of water. It was not necessary to make much allowance for the tide as there is little tidal change in the Indian Ocean.

They explored the island and were amazed at the wide variety of flora and fauna that thrived on this tropical island paradise. In the evening they sat in the cockpit, sipping chilled wine, as they watched the huge orange sun slip below the horizon and sink into the ocean.

The following day Jamie decided to sail off from their anchorage without the assistance of the engine, something he would do with his father when the winds were favourable and they wanted to save the cost of fuel. He raised the sails and left them to luff up windward while he went forward to raise the anchor, leaving Rachel at the helm.

Once the anchor was on deck and secured he returned to the cockpit, pulling in the main sheet first and then the gib sheet. He asked Rachel to point the head of the yacht just off windward and as she did, the sails filled. *Ocean Dream* lurched a little to port and they were off, both sails filled and took the shape of an aeroplane's wing, as they should. Jamie was delighted with the steadiness of the yacht through the water.

They were heading for Praslin, the second largest island. It was not long before they were to see the twin islands of Cousin and Cousine and as they passed close to them, Rachel studied the huge number of coconut groves and the lush vegetation through the binoculars. Praslin had the most stunning beaches they had ever seen on their travels. The brilliant sun reflected the golden colour of the sand as the turquoise waters lapped the foreshore; beyond the beaches were the lush green hills and more palms and coconut trees.

The neighbouring island to Praslin was La Digue where it seemed to Jamie and Rachel that time had stood still. The main form of transport was either the traditional ox cart or the bicycle. They had come to this island to see the giant tortoises and remains of the past, including a magnificent Creole mansion.

Their sailing tour ended with a visit to the coral islands of Bird and Denis, to photograph the rare species of colourful bird life for which these islands were renowned. Rachel loved watching the nesting turtles while Jamie was more interested in the sea life. He wished he had taken the opportunity to include the subaqua equipment offered with the yacht; instead he was having to rely on his snorkel, which still gave him plenty to observe in these clear waters.

These last two weeks had brought him and Rachel even closer together and the dangers that he was aware of back in

England were a dim memory. He had not given much thought to marriage in the past; he was quite happy with the way things were between them. They were both committed to their working professions and gave little thought towards the future. Until now, that was, Jamie thought as his mortality was starting to become a reality.

* * *

They were sitting in the cockpit of the yacht on the last evening of their charter having finished the meal that Rachel had prepared, enjoying a liqueur as a single candle flickered in the breeze. They watched the sun disappear slowly into the ocean and Jamie felt that this might be an ideal moment to approach Rachel on the subject of marriage.

As Jamie added some more liqueur to their glasses he said, 'Do you know, Rachel, this is the longest time we have been alone together since we met.'

'That's funny, Jamie, because I was just thinking the same thing and it's also the most activity we have participated in together.'

'Do you think we could continue this "passing time together" for longer than two weeks?'

'What do you mean, Jamie?'

'Well, we have been an item, as such, for over five years now and never discussed taking our relationship further, into a more permanent situation.'

'You mean living together?'

'Well, sort of ...'

'What do you mean, "sort of"? Do you mean marriage?'

'Well, why not, Rachel?'

'Are you proposing to me, Jamie?'

'I guess I am really – what do you think?'

'I have obviously thought about it, Jamie, but I've been told that to approach the subject before the man you love is ready to propose is the quickest way to end a relationship. I did think that we would reach this point eventually.'

'Does that mean you accept my proposal?'

'Yes, I guess it does.'

'*Yippeeeeeeeeeeeee ...*'

Jamie's response was to lean forward and kiss her passionately; her reply was equally inviting as she felt his hand slide down her back to unfasten the clasp of her bikini. As he caressed her breasts he could feel the nipples were hard and firm; he kissed her neck before lowering his head to take the large dark nipple fully into his mouth. Rachel let out a gentle moan of pleasure and ran her hand over his hair, pushing his head closer to her breast.

Jamie could not wait to remove the bikini bottoms and simply moved them to one side as he entered her. She felt him inside her, filling her completely and holding him tightly she whispered, 'Don't make me wait, Jamie, I need you now – now darling.'

Jamie drove deeper inside her, feeling the pressure of her fingernails between his shoulder blades, and as she arched toward him, his vision exploded with myriad lights and cries of release. While their love juices mingled, their throbbing bodies relaxed and they bonded into one.

Sleep overcame them and they curled themselves together as the twilight deepened into tropical night ...

8 The Wedding

AMIE HAD NO IDEA what he might expect on his return to England. If the 'Woman in Black' was still determined to get her hands on the watch then his and Rachel's lives and their wedding plans could be turned upside down and ruined, so they agreed to get married here on the beach and spend their honeymoon on one of the 'paradise' islands. Rachel was left to investigate the marriage requirements while Jamie organised the honeymoon. After obtaining the document outlining the requirements for marrying in the Seychelles, Rachel went to the hotel's head receptionist, Mandy, who arranged for them to consult the manager. With their help she started her list of essentials, which she now read out to Jamie.

'We will have to visit the civil status office in Victoria to register some details about the wedding. The hotel manager says that we should have given two month's notice but that they can bypass that rule by having the wedding at the hotel. The eleven days' advance notice can also be cut down to two by obtaining a special licence. But we do have one problem, Jamie ... we must produce copies of our birth certificates.'

'No problem for me,' Jamie replied. 'I always carry at least one copy that has been stamped and certified for travelling, in case I lose my passport.'

'Great, I do the same,' exclaimed Rachel. 'Our passports are in the hotel safe, so that part is covered . How are you getting on with our honeymoon arrangements?'

'I'm just about to decide on the island. I think you'll like Bird Island, all I have to do is charter a boat to get us there and back again.'

'Oh Jamie, that sounds wonderful,' said Rachel as she kissed him. 'I'm off to go shopping with Liz.'

'What, the chambermaid?'

'Yes dear, after all she's going to be my bridesmaid!'

After a tour of the local shops, Rachel returned to the hotel with the best that Victoria's boutiques could supply. Everything for their special day seemed to come together very easily.

With Liz the maid as her bridesmaid, Rachel was quite radiant as she made her way down the beach to stand with Jamie and Richard, the hotel manager who was acting as best man. The couple stood under an arbour of tropical flowers in the early morning sunlight, while a minister and the registrar from Victoria performed the service.

The hotel guests had all gathered in the dining room, where the hotel had provided a wedding breakfast and they now crowded round to wish the happy pair all the best in the world. A local three-piece band played their version of the wedding march and the atmosphere was terrific.

A little while later Tony, the manager of the boat hire company, came in his launch to whisk them away to Bird Island, while the hotel staff and its guests continued the party.

9　𝕷𝖔𝖈𝖆𝖙𝖊𝖉

J UST OFF Kensington High Street in a luxury apartment Max was reading *Der Speigel* while he waited for Hans to return from a six kilometre run. Max preferred to do his workout in the apartment's gym: running around in this dreadful English weather and trying to avoid the crowds of people never suited him.

Hans was not the partner he would have chosen to be paired with for this assignment – he was too soft and gutless when things started to get rough; it was his soft background that made him the way he was: his wealthy family protected him from anything they felt might be dangerous and their obsession with the Kaiser was past and old-fashioned. As far as Max was concerned, Hitler was always the true leader, that's why his Nazi party continued after his death, despite the efforts made by Zionist sympathisers.

The apartment's door closed loudly as Hans entered the room; the track suit he wore showed sweat stains down the back and on the chest. He was breathing hard from running up the stairs to the apartment. He removed the tracksuit and threw it into the washing machine on his way through the flat and he entered the shower / wet room as the telephone let out a loud continuous ringing.

Max seemed to take ages to put his newspaper down and raise himself from the armchair to answer the wall phone. When Hans returned to the lounge after his shower, Max was still standing by the phone and writing something on a notepad. He was speaking in German and the conversation seemed very heated. When he finally slammed the receiver back on its cradle, Hans asked,

'Who was that?'

'Erika, who else? She's complaining because we have lost sight of the Irishman. She's getting some grief from her superiors. They do not tolerate failure and our instructions are to get what they want or face the consequences, which would be an example to the rest of the party. They added that 'the Fûhrer never accepted failure and neither will they.'

'What were you writing on the telephone pad?'

'The address of the Irishman's woman. Erika thinks that the watch may be hidden there, or if not, then we take the woman as hostage until he hands over the watch. You drive, Hans. I hate driving in this country, the roads are too small – there are too many cars – and they drive on the wrong side!'

At Rachel's house they gutted the place, just for the pleasure of it. They were pretty sure the watch wasn't there so they smashed everything; it gave them great satisfaction and made them feel important and powerful.

While Hans was taking a break he noticed the Kuoni holiday brochure with some handwriting scribbled over it; he called out to Max and between them they deduced that the Irishman and his woman had escaped them by flying off to the Seychelles. They immediately reported to Erika, who instructed them to follow the pair to the Seychelles and book into the same hotel.

'When you get there, search their rooms,' she said, 'and if necessary torture the woman, in front of the man and get that watch. Kill the girl if you want but don't kill the man until you have the watch in your hands.'

Jamie and Rachel were so happy enjoying their idyllic honeymoon on the beautiful, peaceful island. There were so few people on the island that it seemed, at times, as if they were alone with the natural life of colourful birds and the giant tortoises moving slowly and sleepily around. They felt as if they didn't have a care in the world and they never spoke of their work or the evil pocket watch.

However, it was now time to return to Mahé and the hotel. Tony arrived with the launch to transport them to the bay of the hotel where the hotel manager and Liz, their chambermaid, were waiting for them. Rachel noticed that Liz looked as if she had been crying and they did not seem to be tears of joy. Richard was quick to welcome them back to the shore at the same time, apologising for some sad news that was causing Liz to cry even harder.

'What is it?' Jamie asked in earnest.

'It's your room, sir.'

'What's wrong with our room?' demanded Rachel.

'Well, when Liz entered your room this morning to prepare it for your return, it had been ransacked completely. This has never happened at this hotel before, so I called the police. They are waiting for you now; they want a list of the missing items and they have sealed your room. That is why Liz is so upset: she couldn't prepare it nicely for your return from honeymoon.'

Rachel put her arm around Liz to try and console her, saying that it was not her fault. She then went on to tell her about their wonderful honeymoon to calm her down.

Jamie took less that ten minutes to look around the room and check that there was nothing missing. He identified the culprits' trademarks immediately from his father's and his own trashed apartments.

He informed the police that there was nothing missing but that he would like to get the next available flight to England to save his bride from further upset.

'That will be no problem,' the policeman replied. 'If you will just sign my report and get your things together, I will take you and your wife to the airport in my police car.'
This was the first time anyone had referred to Rachel as his wife. He liked the sound of it and it made him feel very protective towards her. Luck suddenly seemed to be on their side and within a very short time they were on a plane on their way home.

'They have gone,' shouted Max. 'They have left in that police car, we must find out where he's taken them.'

'What? We'd draw attention to ourselves as responsible for wrecking their room.'

'No, of course not. We can casually ask the waitress at dinner this evening.' Max was thinking that Hans could be incredibly stupid at times.

When they learned that their quarry had returned to England, they were thrown into a blind panic, the plan of abducting them and forcing them to reveal the whereabouts of the watch had now been foiled. They were in no hurry to inform Erika of their mistake in wrecking the hotel room and betraying their presence on the island. If only they had simply searched it, they could have watched and waited for the right moment to carry out their duty.

'We must get back to England and complete the job there.'

They were not as fortunate as Jamie and Rachel: it was another four days before they could leave the island.

Rachel was devastated when she saw how badly her home had been vandalised. Every piece of furniture had been damaged and her wall paintings and pictures, thrown onto the floor and smashed. The police were only interested in completing their report and issuing a receipt for anything missing. It was just another statistic as far as they were concerned.

Jamie was more worried about Rachel's safety than the damage and mess. He therefore wasted no time in getting her personal requirements together and driving over to her relative in the East End of London. They remained there for the following week while Jamie reviewed their situation.

After thinking everything through and talking his ideas over with Rachel, they agreed that rather than dealing with the local police Jamie would try to get some attention and support from a more senior authority in the police force. West Central Police Station had an excellent reputation for dealing with crime and taking direct action, and with Rachel's agreement Jamie decided to approach them.

Jamie was now seriously concerned for his welfare, these neo-Nazis were behaving true to their past reputation. It was definitely time to seek some support and protection and he decided to tell them everything about the watch and the circumstances that had arisen since he came into possession of it. It would not be wise to drive into west London by car as it would be too easy for them to identify it and follow him. It would be equally risky if he took a taxi; he decided that the safest way was by public transport.

As he left the underground at Oxford Circus he was sure that he had not been followed. Entering the police station made

Jamie feel uncomfortable and slightly guilty of something he had not done. Perhaps police stations are made to make people feel like this, he thought as he waited to be introduced to a detective sergent who would listen to his problem

Chief Detective Inspector Wingard was over six feet tall, with the physique of an all-England rugby player. His thick brown moustache supported a broken nose and his steel blue eyes made most criminals feel uncomfortable, guilty and willing to confess to anything. Just the sort of policeman Jamie was searching for.

The inspector removed his Harris Tweed jacket and placed it over the back of the chair he was going to sit in, facing Jamie across the interview table. He then placed a file on the table in front of him. This action caused Jamie to raise an eyebrow and wonder what it contained.

'I've been wondering how long it would be before you contacted my office. You and your wife seem to appear and disappear just when I am about to call you in for questioning.'

Jamie was now wondering what he had done and what he was guilty of, that he had to be 'called in for questioning'. It sounded ominous and he was now thinking that perhaps it was not such a good idea to have come here.

Wingard looked at Jamie with ice-cold blue eyes and said, 'Carry on then, what have you got to say?'

Jamie had been knocked completely sideways by this unexpected reception and was feeling totally confused. It took a few minutes and some deep breaths before he could answer. Then he began his story from the moment of his father's death and the legacy of the cursed pocket watch.

'Right,' Wingard replied. 'I know most of that, it's contained in this file,' tapping the documents in front of him. 'How many of the people that are interested in this watch do you know?'

'Only the "Woman in Black", who I met in Vienna.

'Mmm, Erika Von Ritter, if I'm not mistaken.' Opening the file, Wingard began to read. 'She was a high-ranking officer in the British neo-Nazi terrorist group "Fourth Reich" until she failed to murder the Spanish Judge Baltasar Garzón, who was attempting to extradite August Pinochet from Britain. Her ruthless attempts to liquidate the judge were neutralised by the co-operation between the FBI and Scotland Yard, plus the Spanish and Dutch police. This resulted in her being demoted by the Party. She bitterly resented this disgrace, blaming everyone else for the failure of the judge's execution and promptly defected from the neo-Nazis and joined the "Sons of the Gestapo."'

Wingard paused to light his pipe. 'Knowing the motto of the Gestapo – "Death before dishonour" – failure means death.'

Aromatic smoke issued from the pipe .

'Her first assignment for them was your father's pocket watch.'

As he became aware of the background of the 'Woman in Black', a chill went down his spine and his left leg started gyrating uncontrollably. He pressed his hand onto his knee in an attempt to control the spasms.

'You need not fear for your own life. While you have the watch and no-one else knows where it is, you must be kept alive.' Wingard casually informed him. 'Of course, once it's in her hands – she'll kill you.'

This cool assessment of the situation did nothing to calm Jamie' fears and the spasms started again.

The inspector fiddled with his pipe and continued. 'The real danger, as I see it, is for your wife. They will kidnap her and hold her to ransom for the watch. That will be their next move. That is why I have posted a couple of my men at her grandfather's place in the East End. Yes, Mr O'Byrne, I know she's with Mr Kossoff.'

Jamie felt sick. He thought his Rachel was safe but now she was involved to the point of danger and he felt it was all his fault.

'What do I do then?' Jamie asked.

'We have been watching these two groups for some time and so far only been able to neutralise their activities without bringing any charges against them. They are very careful and we also need to pinpoint the leaders. The small fry that carry out the actions will not give us the results we really need to stop any ongoing terrorist activity.'

'Well, where do I stand in all this, ' asked Jamie.

'I need to find out who Erika is taking her orders from in this country and as long as she is interested in you, you are my link to finding out who her boss is.'

'So ....what do I do?' asked Jamie again.

'You do not have to *do* anything, Mr O'Byrne. Just carry on normally and we shall continue to keep a cover on you, until the time is right for us to strike.'

'How long will that be?'

'I can't be definite but not very long,' was Wingard's reply.

'What if I give the watch to you?' Jamie suggested.

'That would be like signing your own death warrant – yours and your wife's. Once they know that you are of no further use to them they will dispose of you. You know what they are after and you have met Erika von Ritter: she has orders to eliminate you both in order to get that watch ... where is the watch by the way?'

'It is in a safe at my company's headquarters.'

'That's great, leave it there. If you do eventually reveal its whereabouts, they will attempt to break in to steal it and my men will be waiting for them.' Tapping the dottle from his pipe

Wingard prepared to end the interview. 'Well, I think we have covered everything so far. Is there anything else you would like to know, Mr O'Byrne? ... Maybe you'd like a cup of tea or coffee?'

'No thanks. I think I need something stronger than tea or coffee at this moment.'

As Jamie left, Wingard passed him his card. 'You can call me any time, day or night and remember that my men will be keeping a watch over you. Ha, excuse the pun! So do not concern yourself over ... Fraulein von Ritter.'

10   Sons of the Gestapo

JAMIE DEPARTED from the building feeling even more anxious than on his arrival. The answers he had hoped for were not forthcoming from Wingard. Despite his assurances of having 'minders', Jamie felt insecure and in danger. As he made his way back to Oxford Circus underground station from Saville Row, he was hoping to pass a pub where he could sustain himself with something stronger than the tea Wingard had offered. As he entered Conduit Street leading to Regent Street, he hardly registered the black Mercedes with tinted windows that slowed to a walking pace beside him.

Just as he turned to look at the car he felt the sudden prick of a hypodermic needle in his buttocks, and at the same time his body went limp. All sound around him diminished as his vision blurred and his legs gave way under him. The door of the car opened and he was physically thrown into the rear of it where Hans was ready to drag him in. Max then got into the car, pinning Jamie to the floor; he was now being held in position by the feet of the two men.

Erika increased the speed of the Merc and eased into the heavy traffic as they made their way south of the river, towards Piccadilly, round Hyde Park, past Buckingham Palace and onwards to the Houses of Parliament. They passed Big Ben and surged over Westminster Bridge. South of the river they headed east to Tooley Street and finally stopped outside a disused warehouse near Butler's Wharf.

* * *

As Jamie started to come round from the knockout injection of Pentathol, ice-cold water was thrown into his face. He was sitting in a solid wood, carver type, chair. His arms were secured by ropes to the chair arms and a similar wooden chair had been laid on it's back in front of him and his legs had been bound to the solid chair legs with more rope, so that he could not move. A powerful desk lamp was directed onto his face, which made it impossible for him to focus when he opened his eyes. When he looked up he felt an iron-hard fist connect sharply with his jaw, which split his lip. He could feel a trickle of warm blood run down his chin.

'That's to let you know, Mr O'Byrne, that we mean business. You will not leave here until we have the Fuhrer's watch in our hands.'

This was spoken in a clear Germanic accent and Jamie guessed that the two dark shadows moving around on the borders of the light must be working for the Woman in Black, whom Wingard had named as Erika von Ritter. Max was the aggressive interrogator while Hans remained quietly in the background.

Suddenly Jamie felt a huge hand grab the back of his hair, painfully pulling his head backwards to face the ceiling.

Max's ugly face came into his vision as he shouted, 'You can hear me, can't you, Mr O'Byrne? Unless you start to answer me, I will have to let Hans have his "fun" with you, just as he did with the old Jewish pawnbroker.'

Jamie was experiencing a mixture of fear and confusion. He had no idea how to respond to the situation he was in ! So much for Detective Inspector Wingard's 'minders'!

'He is refusing to talk, Hans ... It's up to you to loosen his tongue.'

Hans moved closer to Jamie so that he could see him clearly; he was slapping the rubber tube into the palm of his left hand, and standing only inches away from Jamie's bare feet he said, 'This is something you will not enjoy, so I shall leave it until later ... in the meantime I will give you another treat to help you answer Max's questions.'

Hans moved quickly away and reappeared with some toothpicks; grabbing Jamie' feet he forced these under the nails of each toe, one by one. The pain was excruciating for Jamie and he felt his legs shaking with pain.

'You have heard of acupuncture, haven't you, Mr O'Byrne. Well, this is my version. As I activate each of these little sticks, your tongue will become looser and the saliva will help you to answer the questions.'

Jamie knew that once they had obtained the watch from the Hilton Hotel Group's headquarters, he would be 'finished off' by them and he had no way of informing Wingard that they were about to steal the watch. His thoughts turned to Rachel, hoping that she was safe. For some reason he remembered how often she jokingly reminded him that it was only women who could multitask – men couldn't do it – she would tease.

If that's true, he thought, *how am I thinking of Rachel and getting this pain at the same time?*

However, the more he concentrated on Rachel, the less pain he felt. So he started to fix his mind, as if in a trance, on their wonderful holiday and wedding in the Seychelles. Using every tiny moment they shared as a barrier against the torture.

'This is having no effect,' Max shouted at Hans.

'These things take time,' Hans replied, 'but I am always successful in the end. If we do it your way and he dies before we have the watch, we would have failed Erika and the Party. You know the Party's policy for failure. It would be *us* floating in the

River Thames. Remember, as far as we're concerned, he's the only one who knows where the Fuhrer's watch is hidden.'

Hans then struck a match and started to light each of the toothpicks, as if they were candles on a birthday cake. They burned down one by one onto Jamie's bleeding toenails; the pain was so much worse than before, making Jamie concentrate even harder on Rachel and the Seychelles.

While all this was happening, Max continued to repeat the questioning.

'Where is the watch? Where have you hidden it?'

'You must increase the pain on this stubborn *Schwein*. Loosen his tongue, damn you,' Max shouted, 'or leave him to me.'

'I will leave him to you when we have the watch and not before. I remember what happened the last time I left a prisoner to you. He died before we had the information we wanted. We cannot make that mistake this time.'

Changing tactics, Hans grabbed up the rubber tube and swiped it across the sole of Jamie's right foot.

The scream rang through the rafters of the warehouse and Jamie's body arched against the ropes that held him.

'That seems more effective,' Max informed Hans in a matter of fact way. 'Again,' he ordered.

Hans repeated the punishment, with the left foot, shouting, 'Left, right, left, right, that's how you British march, isn't it, Mr O'Byrne?'

Despite the pain, Jamie continued to say nothing and doubled his efforts in thinking of Rachel. Each blow with the rubber tube was causing involuntary movements in Jamie and he felt sure that the wooden arms of the chair were loosening in their joints. Suddenly the loud shrill ring of a telephone echoed through the warehouse.

'That will be Erika,' Max exclaimed, as he left to walk the seventy-five metres to the small office where the telephone was connected. Hans was not distracted from administering his punishment, until Max shouted from the office that Erika wanted to speak with him as well.

As Hans walked away from him, Jamie pulled against the arms of the chair, lifting them from their joints. He slipped his arms out of their restraints and quickly bent to release his legs. He knew he had to get out of the light – one of them might see him and foil his attempt to escape – but his feet were swollen and bloody. He realised that he was not going to be able to get far. The huge metal warehouse door, large enough for vehicles to pass through, was about twenty-five metres away. Within this expanse of metal was the smaller exit door and he knew that this was his only hope.

As he placed his bare feet on the stone floor he only just stifled a cry. His feet were so badly damaged that he would never escape and those two evil bastards would catch him and continue their torture. Hobbling across to the small door, he pulled it open, then slammed it again with all his remaining strength, the loud metallic bang echoed from the door, pulsating into the darkness. Jamie then shuffled over to the high stacked pallets to the right of the door. These had been placed about half a metre out from the wall, leaving just enough space for him to squeeze into and hide behind them.

Max and Hans raced out of the small office, took one look at the damaged chair in its pool of light and started screaming at each other in German. They ran to the warehouse door and as they stepped outside, Jamie could hear Max ordering Hans to take the car and go to the right while he would run in the opposite direction.

Jamie thanked his lucky stars that he had so little room to move, otherwise he would have slumped to the ground. Instead he clung to the pallets and rested his head against them. He had intended to wait for around ten minutes to let them get far enough away, before he made his move to leave the warehouse, lose himself in the shadows and make his way back to Rachel but the condition of his feet made that an almost impossible dream.

Damn it, think man, think, was all that kept going through his head. The shock of the small door being flung open and dark shadows entering with torches and machine guns really blew his mind. The figures positioned themselves around the warehouse and a voice whispered into the darkness.

'All clear and secure, sir,' and the huge figure of Detective Inspector Wingard entered the warehouse.

From his hiding place Jamie gasped and shouted out, 'It's about time you arrived!' but the click of the machine gun clips being pulled back silenced him.

'Hands on your head,' was the order as the man by the door pointed the machine gun towards him.

'Hold, that will not be necessary,' Wingard informed the man.

'What happened to the protection you promised me?' demanded Jamie.

'You were followed on foot from my office but the two officers assigned to you did not expect you to be bundled into a car that they couldn't pursue. They got the reg number but it has taken until now to establish the last sighting of the car. Let's get you out of here and attend to those feet, they look a mess.'

Typical unruffled, matter of fact, bloody DCI Wingard, thought Jamie.

After he had seen the doctor and the medication had been applied to his feet, he was taken in an unmarked car to Rachel's grandfather's house in the East End. She and her grandfather were shocked to hear of Jamie's terrible experience but so pleased that he was safe again. The additional information offered to Jamie by Wingard was equally interesting.

'What are your next plans, Jamie?' asked old Mr Kossoff.

'Well, DCI Wingard has told me to sit tight here until I hear from him. Neither Rachel nor I should leave the house, which is being watched by two of his "reliable" officers ... I hope they are better than the last lot! The immediate future is something I must discuss with Rachel before I make my next move.'

It was to be a week of constant care before Jamie's feet returned to normal and he could start wearing shoes instead of slippers. During this week he was able to discuss the next step of resolving the disposal of the watch – once and for all.

Max and Hans had been informed, in no uncertain terms, by Erika von Ritter, that their inability to obtain any information about the location of the watch had been noted and their usefulness to the organisation was close to being terminated – permanently.

They had allowed the prisoner to escape and despite the torturous punishment, they said they had inflicted on him, he had been able to get away from them, on foot, without being caught.

'We are in trouble, thanks to you,' Max informed Hans. 'You should have made sure the Irishman could not escape before you came to the phone.'

'And you should have replaced me, by keeping watch on him, instead of staying near the phone so you didn't miss anything,' countered Hans.

'Either way,' Max replied, 'we are in serious trouble. We both know how members of the Party are dealt with – when they fail. Erika will not take any of the blame herself, so it is up to us to make sure the next contact with the Irishman is the last one and we get the watch.'

'Erika said the only way to get the information we need is through his woman,' was Hans reply.

'How so?' queried Max.

'We direct the punishment on her, in front of him, he will feel guilty that he is inflicting the pain on her by not giving us the information we want, and give in.'

'That's fine,' said Max, 'but it means that we need to kidnap two prisoners, when we cannot even get our hands on one! All we can do is wait, here in this apartment, until we hear from Erika.'

11 Options

JAMIE WAS getting frustrated with being cooped up, like a pigeon, in Aaron Kossof's tiny cottage. He had fully recovered his fitness and was keen to put an end to this 'pocket watch' business and start his married life with Rachel. He had lost confidence in Wingard and his men, who had so easily lost contact with him, when he was kidnapped. He was trying hard to concentrate on some alternatives for the disposal of the watch, which might satisfy his father's wishes and protect both him and Rachel at the same time.

Ireland kept intruding into his thoughts as he was considering some ideas, until finally he said out loud, 'Well, why not? That could well be the solution I am looking for and meet all the criteria at the same time.'

'What is that?' Rachel asked, looking up from the book she was reading.

'It's only an idea. What if I returned the watch to my father, in Ireland?'

'Oh darling, how can you do that? He's dead,' she sighed.

'I know, but what if I went back to his grave and buried the watch with him? I could tell him over the grave that Manny is dead and I cannot find another Jew to accept the watch. He would not want me to keep the watch, if it could endanger my life.'

'Would you ask Wingard to escort you to Ireland, for security?'

'I don't think so. His protection so far has not been very good and anyway his men might attract unwanted attention from those two "Sons of the Gestapo". No. I think I would do better on my own.'

'How will you be able to leave here and get to your head office in Watford to collect the watch? Then you've got to get to the Holyhead Ferry crossing without Wingard's men catching up with you.'

'If my kidnappers were able to slip past them, then I'm sure I can, as well. Three heads are better than one – let's make a plan.'

* * *

The next morning their plan was put into action. Rachel and her grandfather went to the front door where they were soon joined by Wingard's two 'minders'. They engaged in discussion about how all three of them had been cooped up like pigeons in this cottage for over a week. They wanted Wingard to come and tell them how much longer he expected them to remain virtually captive.

Meanwhile Jamie had slipped into the back garden, climbed over the neighbour's wall into the rear alleyway and was making his way to Rachel's car. He then drove back to Commercial Road and into the heavy morning traffic, heading towards the M1 motorway and Watford where, in the Hilton Hotel's head office, the watch was locked in a safe.

When Jamie arrived at the office, the security guard on the gate informed him that everyone had been asking after him: no-one had seen him since his visit to Vienna. He told Jamie that he had orders to direct him to the Director's office as soon as he 'showed his nose'. Jamie thought about ignoring this and just getting the watch and heading off to Holyhead, but remembered that he had marked the packet 'Security/Confidential' and as such, it would need the approval of the Director for release.

He called in at the Head of Security's office asking if he could just take the packet, only to be informed that it was not possible – 'Not without permission from above, guv.'

Idiot, thought Jamie, as he took the lift to the seventh floor but then rules were there for good reasons. He was wondering how he was to explain his absence and also avoid drawing his boss into the danger and problems that surrounded the legacy left to him by his father.

The Director's secretary gave Jamie a look of despair. 'We have all been wondering what had happened to you. The boss is not very happy with you so you'd better have a good excuse for your absence without leave!'

She buzzed the inter-office phone and informed the Director that Jamie had arrived.

'Send him in immediately,' Jamie overheard him say.

'Come in, Jamie, and take a seat. Are you OK? We've all been very puzzled by your absence – no fax or phone message. I was so concerned I sent one of the lads to your apartment for an answer but there was no reply. I was on the verge of informing the police about your disappearance.'

'That won't be necessary, George. It was a domestic, family matter, that developed after the death of my father. I should have contacted you and I apologise for not doing so. All my concentration was taken up with the situation I was facing and time seemed to slip by.'

'Would you like to talk to me about it, Jamie? As you know I have always been willing to help by adopting an "open door" policy with every member of my staff.'

'I really appreciate your offer, George, but it's a family matter that can only be resolved by the family. That is why I have come to ask if you would agree for me to extend my absence for one further week. I need to return to Ireland to bring the situation to an end.'

'Take as long as you have to, Jamie, but do keep me up to date and let me know when you'll be back.'

'Thanks, George, I have to collect a packet from Security which needs your approval for release.'

'No worries, Jamie.' The Director lifted the handset to inform Security of his approval. 'Off you go and good luck.'

Jamie stood to leave and shook the Director's outstretched hand.

'By the way, Jamie, that marketing exercise you carried out in Vienna was excellent. We have put it into action and are already getting favourable reports back.'

Jamie collected the watch from Security and signed the receipt for the guard, who mumbled, 'I was only doing my job, sir.'

Jamie looked him in the eye, saying,. 'It's not always what we do, but the way we do it ...' and left.

12   𝕽oots?

As Jamie made his way through the heavy traffic on the A41 to pick up the M40 to Birmingham, he hoped he would be in time for the ferry to Ireland. He had to negotiate Spaghetti Junction and get to Chester and North Wales on the M6 and from there to Anglesey and the road to Holyhead; he was now so stressed and anxious about the watch that he did not want to lose a minute in getting shot of it.

A night in Holyhead held no pleasure for him. There was no available car space on any ferry, so Jamie booked himself into the Hotel Kingsland for the night because it was the nearest hotel to the ferry port. He had reserved a place for Rachel's car on the next available ferry, which was sailing at 8.20 the following morning with an expected arrival time of 11.35.

At 7.30 the next morning Max had just started his breakfast when the phone rang. He was contemplating whether to answer it or leave it for Hans to answer, but as there was no movement from the bathroom, he threw his spoon into his muesli, muttered 'Damn it' and walked over to the wallphone.

It was Erika von Ritter to inform him that Jamie O'Byrne had just boarded the Irish ferry at Holyhead which was due to dock in Dun Laoghaire at 11.35. A private plane was waiting for him and Hans at Heathrow Airport to get them into Dublin Airport before the ferry docked. A car would be available for them and he was told to write down the details of the car that Jamie was driving. She was sure that he had the watch with him, they need only finish him off, take the watch, get back to the private plane which would wait for them, and meet her in the apartment.

'This is a simple, straightforward operation,' Erika informed him, 'even for you two. I do not want any mistakes, excuses are not acceptable. Do not carry your guns or knives with you – the airport checks would discover them. These will be provided for you. When you go to pick up the car, check that the guns and ammunition are in the luggage compartment before you take over the car. Do *not* return without that watch!'

The ferry crossing was as rough as ever. When the Atlantic meets the Irish Sea, turbulent waves make the three-hour crossing, on these flat-keeled ferries, very uncomfortable. Many of the passengers were seasick during the trip, and although Jamie was fortunately not one of them, the journey nevertheless seemed interminable.

At 11.40 the ship's Tannoy system informed all drivers and their passengers to return to their vehicles and all foot passengers to stand by to vacate the vessel.

Jamie started the car and waited for the Land Rover in front of him to move away and, as he followed it, a surge of adrenalin ran through his body. He was convinced that what he was about to do was the right thing and that his father would have understood. At the time he was given the watch, his father had no idea of the danger he was placing into Jamie's hands. He had simply asked his son to return the watch to old Manny Rosenberg.

Jamie had no idea whether burying the watch in his father's grave, and honouring his father's dying wish in his own way, would protect him from his fate at the hands of the two villains. How much protection he could expect from Detective Inspector

Wingard was doubtful, so he had to consider seriously how he could protect Rachel and himself after he buried the watch.

The Land Rover moved away slowly and Jamie followed at the same speed until he was out of Dun Laoghaire. The two and a half hour drive to Glenamaddy would take him onto the N31 to avoid the M50 motorway round Dublin; then on to the Barn Hill Crossroads and back onto the R148 to Mullingar. A short time ago he had made this journey to attend his sister's wedding; it was almost impossible to believe all the things that had happened since then, but he could not visit the family again until this madness was ended.

He cleared his mind and concentrated on the driving; he would cope with things to the best of his ability. He could do no more.

Hans and Max arrived at Dublin Airport in good time and had no difficulty meeting up with their contact in the car park. Max was not pleased with the red BMW sports car they were supplied with, and remonstrated with his compatriot in German, complaining at the lack of common sense in providing them with such a high-profile car for surveillance work. They could be so easily identified at any distance and they would be unable to lose themselves in a flow of traffic. To use that awful English phrase – they would stick out like a sore thumb!

The car supplier said that he was instructed to provide a car of sufficient speed to enable them to keep up with their target. As he was not informed of the type of car they were to follow, he had obtained the fastest car he could get at short notice.

Hans had a complaint of his own. The guns supplied were Smith & Wesson instead of the Mausers which he and Max were specially trained to use. The Mauser C96, that Max favoured, was a powerful, field handgun that could be upgraded to a rifle, with the addition of a stock; it normally contained up to twenty rounds of ammunition. Hans always used the lighter and smaller Mauser HSc with eight rounds.

Hans was told that the Smith & Wesson 500PC, Comped Hutner revolver had a 7½ in barrel and was designed for hunting and was very powerful with a good range. The other gun that had been provided was a .44 revolver by the same manufacturer, small and lightweight with a two inch snub barrel.

'Yes ... and they only hold five rounds each as opposed to the eight plus rounds ... plus the fact that we have never used either of these guns before.'

Their contact shrugged his shoulders, replying, 'As far as I have been told, your target does not have a gun to defend himself. With this car, you should be near enough to hit him over the head with your guns, if you run out of bullets.'

Max and Hans did not appreciate the fellow's humour and busied themselves checking the guns and additional ammunition, before studying the map and directions to Glenamaddy. They agreed the route and Max squeezed his huge frame into the driving seat of the sports car and adjusted the seat and all the mirrors. He took a spin round the car park to get the feel of the car. Hans took his seat and they drove off, making for Dun Laoghaire and the ferry port.

They arrived as the vessel docked and had a good vantage point as the cars started to disembark. It was not long before they spotted the target car following a Land Rover off the ferry. They picked up Jamie's route and trailed him at a safe distance. They were not worried about losing him in the traffic because they knew where he was heading; their only concern at this stage was whether he intended to take the motorway or the alternative route which would suit their purposes better. They needed to catch him on a lonely stretch of road to complete the job and get out of Ireland.

Jamie was pleased he had avoided the M50 motorway as the route he had chosen was much more pleasant and enjoyable, despite the heavy rain which was making the leaf-strewn road hazardous on the bends. These conditions needed a light touch on the brake, otherwise you could be in trouble.

He was now joining the N4 to Longford, following the signs for Roscommon; it was on this stretch of the road that he saw the red sports car which he was sure had followed him out of Dublin. He felt it was suspicious and therefore decided to change his planned route to Glenamaddy by taking the R362 instead of the R264 after Roscommon. If the car was still behind him after taking the diversion it would prove that someone was following him and the new route would give him a better chance to lose them.

After Castlecoote the red sports car started to close in on the rear of his car. Jamie knew this route well as he had used it many times in the past, but watching the winding road in this torrential rain and glancing at the rearview mirror so often was making it difficult to shake off his pursuers.

Max shouted at Hans to open the window and shoot out the two rear tyres of the car.

'The rain on my glasses is spoiling my vision,' Hans replied.

'Well, remove your glasses, you idiot.'

'How will I see the tyres without my glasses?'

'Just shoot at the bloody car then and hope to hit something, *Dummkopf!*' Max fought to keep control of the car as the rain slanted down.

Jamie thought he recognised the man leaning out of the passenger window with something waving about in his hand, then came the crack of a pistol shot passing over the top of the car. He ducked automatically, gripped the steering wheel and pushed his foot hard down on the accelerator.

Two more shots passed either side of the car, before another burst the rear near-side tyre, sending the car into a clockwise skid. Jamie found himself facing the red BMW, racing towards him, as his car slid down the side of the muddy road. A head-on collision seemed inevitable but Max pulled the steering wheel to the right, pressing his foot on the brake pedal at the same time.

The car screeched across the road at great speed – smack into a tree. Hans was thrown through the windscreen, headlong into the tree trunk and was killed instantly. Max meanwhile had the wind blown out of his lungs by the collapsible steering wheel and he was so stunned that his mind went blank and he literally saw stars in his eyes.

13   𝕯𝖊𝖘𝖙𝖎𝖓𝖞

AMIE WAS hardly affected by the cartwheel motion of the car and luckily only slid off the road into the mud. However he realised that his car was as immobilised as his attackers and his only chance of escape was across the bogs that he knew so well from his boyhood. He was out of the car in a moment and trotted off into the bogs while Max was slumped over his steering wheel.

Within seconds Max had recovered from the shock of the accident and quickly took stock of the situation. Hans was dead, his body a twisted wreck on the bonnet of the car, his eyes open and staring into space while the rain washed his blood into the fallen leaves.

Max flipped open the glove compartment to reach for the gun but rejected the snub-nose pistol, knowing that he would need a gun with a greater range than it could cover. The gun Hans had used lay in the well of the car and he lifted the Smith & Wesson 500 PC by its 7½ inch barrel, hefted it and checked to see what shells remained. Grabbing a box of 9 mm shells, he reloaded and stuffed the rest in his pocket and stuck the gun in his waistband.

He tried the door but it was jammed shut and would not budge, he had no option but to follow Hans's body through the smashed windscreen.

Jamie had established a good hundred metres' gap between him and the cars before Max started after him, but this advantage was short lived as he became breathless with running and had to slow his pace. Max was much fitter and stronger than Jamie and he began to narrow the distance between them.

It was not long before Jamie was no more than fifty metres ahead of Max. Close enough for him to raise the Smith & Wesson to eye level in the standard two-handed grip to steady the heavy pistol, brace his legs and squeeze the trigger. The recoil was tremendous and the noise nearly shattered his eardrums and Max snorted as the bullet ploughed into the ground at Jamie's feet.

The gap between them had now increased by another ten metres and Max hurried on to reduce it again. When he gauged that Jamie was only forty metres away, he loosed off another two rounds which passed close to his quarry.

'Damned useless,' he grunted. 'If I only had my Mauser he would have been finished by now.'

Max continued to close the gap as Jamie's breathing became painful and he slowed to an almost walking pace. He knew he was nearly finished: this whole episode of his life was soon to be closed as the distance dwindled to twenty-five metres between him and his destiny.

Max stopped and raised the heavy gun once more in the two-handed stance, took a deep breath to steady himself and then fired. By a miracle of chance the bullet missed its target and Max cursed the gun as he took aim again. Jamie no sooner heard the piercing crack than he felt the searing heat of the bullet.

It took him in the pelvis and jammed into the pelvic bone; he hit the ground with a thump as the velocity of the shot in his left side spun him to the right and down into the wet muddy bog. He lay there, unable to move as Max came close to stand over him with the gun in his right hand.

'Where is the watch?' he demanded.

'Go to hell and find it yourself!' Jamie spat out the words.

'That I will do,' Max replied, as he turned Jamie over roughly, while he rifled through his pockets searching for the diabolical watch.

'Ah!' With a final flourish he produced it from the inside pocket of Jamie's mud-splattered jacket. Looking at the swastika on the front of the case with elation, he pressed the button and the lid sprang open, revealing the 18 carat gold watch that he had finally succeeded in obtaining. He closed the case and held it in his left hand.

Looking down at Jamie as he pointed the gun at his head, he said, 'What are your last words, Irishman?'

Jamie could think of nothing of consequence to say other than, 'Thanks for the watch, Da, but I could have done without it.'

Max then pulled the hammer back and squeezed the trigger, only to hear the blank sound of a click.

'Damn this gun,' he muttered, 'only five shells.' He flipped open the chamber and watched as the empty cases fell to the muddy footpath.

At the same time Jamie heard the loud crack of a rifle shot and the mud spurted up as the shot grounded beside Max. Jamie looked in the direction the rifle sound had come from and saw Detective Inspector Wingard standing next to Rachel and a policeman with a high-velocity rifle, with telescopic sight attached, striding towards him.

Max screamed something in German as he turned to run back along the footpath, not realising that in having followed Jamie, who knew the safe passage across the bogs, he had no idea how to negotiate them on his own and without this knowledge there was no way he could retrace his steps with safety.

His pace started to slow as the bog sucked at his feet; as he sank to his knees in the black mess, another loud crack sounded from the rifle and the bullet struck Max square between the shoulder blades, catapulting him forward face down, while the precious watch sprang out of the case to land in front of him.

Max's body started to sink as he struggled to reach out for the elusive watch. Slowly the lower part of his body disappeared until finally, his mouth wide open in a silent scream, his head sank below the muddy swamp. He continued to grab for the watch which lay glinting on top of the ooze, the chain laid out behind it. Max's left forearm was all that could be seen as he continued to grope around with his outstretched hand. Finally his fingers caught the chain and held it high, then his hand sank into the bog, the watch and chain slithering in after him.

Epilogue

Before returning to England, Jamie took Rachel to the cemetery where his father was laid to rest. They were met at the entrance by Father Patrick O'Malley, an old friend of the family.

Jamie and Rachel read the words on the tombstone, then Jamie spoke of his father, saying that although he may not have honoured his father's wishes in the way he had wanted to, in view of the circumstances he felt that he had done his best.

Now the watch was lost at the bottom of the bog that would be the end of the curse of Hitler's pocket watch forever.

'Let us pray that it will be so,' the priest said. 'Although I've heard that there may be plans to drain the bogs in the future…'

Author's note

Adolf Hitler was given a pocket watch by his sister as a birthday present. Later Hitler had several watches made as gifts. One in particular was an 18 ct gold pocket watch, with all the Nazi insignia, for Albert Speer's birthday. It is this watch that inspired this book. It was put up for auction in October 2006 by Minas Katchadorian, a London art dealer and thousands of potential buyers showed interest in the watch. The new owner and the selling price remain a secret.

In many European countries, including Germany, it is illegal to buy, own or sell Nazi memorabilia.

Extract from Raised Bog Restoration document

Raised bogs are rare in the European Union (EU) and are becoming increasing scarce and under threat in Ireland. Raised bogs have been developing in Ireland for thousands of years and once covered over 310,000 ha.

However due to extensive peat harvesting for fuel and horticulture as well as drainage for agriculture and forestry much of the original raised bog habitat has been lost (approx 92%).

9 780956 909848